AS THE KID GOES FOR BROKE

From Washington to California to Peking, it's hard to tell as one follows the fortunes of the DOONESBURY CAST just where the wages of political education are most agonizing...Perhaps on Capitol Hill, where Congressman Ventura must explain what he was doing in a motel with an employee of no known qualifications other than clear diction and admirable posture. Or in Berkeley, where Virginia Slade's run for Congress stumbles over the quaint but effective campaign of a bluestocking Republican WASP. Or perhaps it is most painful in mainland China where Uncle Duke must undergo appendectomy by acupuncture. Wherever, one thing is abundantly clear: the only cartoon strip to win a Pulitzer Prize gets ever more delightfully opportunistic.

DOONESBURY

In just a few years, a remarkable new comic strip called DOONESBURY has provoked more public and media reaction than any cartoon in the last twenty years, winning legions of loyal followers. Michael J. Doonesbury and the denizens of Walden Commune appear in nearly four hundred newspapers with a readership of over 23 million.

As the Kid Goes for Broke

a *Doonesbury* book by G. B. Trudeau

BANTAM BOOKS
TORONTO NEW YORK LONDON

AS THE KID GOES FOR BROKE

A Bantam Book / published by arrangement with
Holt, Rinehart and Winston

PRINTING HISTORY

Holt, Rinehart and Winston edition published October 1977

Bantam edition / February 1979
2nd printing . . . . . July 1980

"DOES EVERYBODY ELSE DO IT?"
IS CAPITOL HILL IN FACT
TEEMING WITH PAYROLLED
NON-TYPISTS?

PIQUED BY HIS TREATMENT BY
THE HOUSE ETHICS COMMITTEE,
CONGRESSMAN VENTURA HAS LEVELED
SERIOUS CHARGES AT HIS PEERS,
STRONGLY IMPLYING THAT THE VAST
MAJORITY ALSO ENGAGE IN QUES-
TIONABLE HIRING PRACTICES.

IS SUCH BEHAVIOR REALLY AS
PREVALENT AS VENTURA CLAIMS?
"60 MINUTES" SET OUT WITH A
CAMERA CREW TO SEE FOR OUR-
SELVES. FIRST STOP: A CON-
GRESSIONAL HOUSEBOAT!

FIRST USED DURING THE
HARDING ADMINISTRATION,
THESE COLORFUL, FLOATING
ALIBIS HAVE DOTTED THE
POTOMAC FOR YEARS..

GBTrudeau

I'M GLAD YOU'RE HERE, BERNIE — WE CAN USE THE REINFORCEMENTS! WE'RE BEING **PLAGUED** BY MURPHY'S LAW!

"IF SOMETHING CAN GO WRONG, IT WILL?"

WITH A VENGEANCE! IN OUR CASE THE UNDERWATER TELEVISION RIG COLLAPSED, THE STROBE UNIT BURNED OUT, OUR TRANSFORMER WAS CONFISCATED AT CUSTOMS, AND OUR DIVER HAS BEEN JAILED FOR PUBLIC DRUNKENNESS!

SO WHAT'RE THEY SAYING ABOUT ME IN THE JOURNALS?

THAT YOU'RE MAD, BUT NOT DANGEROUS.

MR. SANDERSON, YOU'VE BEEN ASSISTANT GARDENER HERE AT THE WHITE HOUSE DURING THE EIGHT YEARS B.J. EDDY WAS HEAD TULIP. HOW DO YOU FEEL ABOUT HIS LEAVING?

WELL, PERSONALLY, ED, I'M REAL SORRY TO SEE HIM GO. B.J. UNDERSTOOD THAT A FLOWER THAT FELT GOOD LOOKED GOOD, SO HE WENT TO GREAT PAINS TO KEEP UP MORALE AND GOOD HUMOR ON THE GROUNDS.

I'LL NEVER FORGET HOW DURING ONE PARTICULARLY DEPRESSING PERIOD, B.J. ARRANGED FOR A ROW OF JONQUILS OUTSIDE THE OVAL OFFICE TO BURST INTO FULL BLOOM IN THE MIDDLE OF JANUARY!

MR. NIXON ORDERED THEM CUT DOWN, OF COURSE, BUT THE GARDEN WAS IN STITCHES FOR WEEKS!

HEE, HEE! THAT'S GREAT!

GBTrudeau

TULIPS, IT SEEMS, COME AND GO, BUT THE DEPARTURE OF B.J. EDDY FROM THE EAST LAWN MARKS THE END OF AN ERA. MORE ON THAT STORY FROM BOB SCHIEFFER.

TO THE THOUSANDS OF BULBS FOR WHOM THE WHITE HOUSE GROUNDS HAVE ALWAYS BEEN HOME, THE HEAD TULIP'S DISMISSAL HAS COME AS SOMETHING OF A SHOCK. FOR IF B.J. EDDY WAS NOTHING ELSE, HE WAS A PERENNIAL'S PERENNIAL.

THE THIRD GENERATION PROGENY OF A PRIZED HYBRID OF AMSTERDAM REDS, EDDY FIRST JOINED THE WHITE HOUSE IN 1967 AS A HOUSE PLANT, WHERE HE WON WIDE RECOGNITION AS AN AGGRESSIVE, EARLY BLOOMER.

REPOTTED DURING THE NIXON ADMINISTRATION..

HEY, **GREAT** COLOR FOOTAGE!

SSSHH!

@BTrudeau